RAIDERS OF VANOK

Raiders of Vanok is a work of fiction. References to real people, events, establishments, organizations, or locales are intended only to provide the sense of authenticity and are use fictitiously. All other characters, all incidents, dialogue are drawn from the author's imagination and are not to be seen as real.

Copyright © 2021 by Ty'Ron W. C. Robinson II. All rights reserved.

Published by Dark Titan Publishing. A division of Dark Titan Entertainment.

Also available in eBook.

Prodigious Worlds is an imprint of Dark Titan Entertainment.

Paperback ISBN: 978-1-7369944-9-8
eBook ISBN: 978-1-7376143-0-2

darktitanentertainment.com

WORKS BY TY'RON W. C. ROBINSON II

BOOKS/SHORT STORIES

DARK TITAN UNIVERSE SAGA

MAIN SERIES
Dark Titan Knights
The Resistance Protocol
Tales of the Scattered
Tales of the Numinous
Day of Octagon
Crossbreed
Heaven's Called
The Oranos Imperative

Forthcoming
Underworld
Magicks and Mysticism
The Resistance vs. The Enforcement Order

SPIN-OFFS
In A Glass of Dawn: The Casebook of Travis Vail
Maveth: Bloodsport
The Curse of The Mutant-Thing

Forthcoming
Trail of Vengeance
War of The Thunder Gods
Maveth vs. The Swordman

ONE-SHOTS
Maveth, The Death-Bringer
Mystery of The Mutant-Thing
Shade & Switchblade
Retribution of Cain
The Mythologists
Ambush Bot
Kang-Zhu

COLLECTIONS
Dark Titan Omnibus: Volume 1
Dark Titan Omnibus: Volume 2
Dark Titan One-Shot Collection

THE HAUNTED CITY SAGA
The Legendary Warslinger: The Haunted City I
Battle of Astolat: A Haunted City Prequel (KOBO Exclusive)
Redemption of the Lost: The Haunted City II
Consequences of the Suffering: The Haunted City III (Forthcoming)

SYMBOLUM VENATORES
Symbolum Venatores: The Gabriel Kane Collection
Hod: A Symbolum Venatores Book
Symbolum Venatores: War of The Two Kingdoms
Symbolum Venatores: Elrad's Chronicles
Symbolum Venatores: Mystery of the Magician (Forthcoming)
Symbolum Venatores: Twilight of the Gods (Forthcoming)

EVERWAR UNIVERSE
EverWar Universe: Knights & Lords
EverWar Universe: The Damned Ones (Forthcoming)

PRODIGIOUS WORLDS
Mark Porter of Argoron
Raiders of Vanok
Praxus of Lithonia (Forthcoming)

FRIGHTENED! SERIES
Frightened!: The Beginning
Frightened!: The Light Sky (Forthcoming)

INSTINCTS SERIES
Lost in Shadows: Remastered
Instincts: Point Hope (Forthcoming)
Shadow in the Mirror: Instincts II (Forthcoming)

CHEVAH MYTHOS
The Eleventh Hour; A Chevah Mythos Story

THE HORDE TRILOGY
The Horde
The Dreaded Ones (Forthcoming)
Our Sealed Fate (Forthcoming)

DARK TITAN'S THE DEAD DAYS
Accounts of The Dead Days
Brand New Day: The Dead Days I (Forthcoming)

OTHER BOOKS
The Book of The Elect
The Extended Age Omnibus
The Supreme Pursuer: Darkness of the Hunt and Other Stories
Massacre in the Dusk (Forthcoming)

THE DARK TITAN AUDIO EXPERIENCE PODCAST
Season 1: Introductions
Season 2: In a Glass of Dawn
Season 2.5: Accounts of The Dead Days
Season 3: Battle For Astolat
Season 4: Hallow Sword: Cursed

RAIDERS OF VANOK

TY'RON W. C. ROBINSON II

CONTENTS

- CHAPTER 1: VANCE HARLAN - 1
- CHAPTER 2: WELCOME ABOARD - 6
- CHAPTER 3: CALYPSO - 11
- CHAPTER 4: THE KINGDOM OF VETORIA - 19
- CHAPTER 5: A TEST OF FORTITUDE AND KNOWLEDGE - 27
- CHAPTER 6: PIRATES OF VANOK - 37
- CHAPTER 7: A WAY HOME? - 41
- CHAPTER 8: THE VANOKIAN PATH - 47

- NEW ORDER OF THE WORLD - 51
- MARK PORTER OF ARGORON EXCERPTS - 64

CHAPTER 1: VANCE HARLAN

As astrologists and astronomers continued their research pertaining to other living beings throughout the universe, Vance Harlan, a man specialized in the scientific community of interstellar space proposed a plan. His plans to travel into the stars through a wormhole, hoping to come out into another galaxy filled with life. Vance pleaded his plans and works to many other scientists. All of whom rejected. Vance even went as far as to proceed with funding for his own ship to travel into space. Backers were not impressed. Stating Vance was living in a fantasy-land hoping to collude with alien beings.

During one meeting with the Department of Defense, Vance entered the room, brushing his blonde hair before seeing it was cornered by guards. He nodded with cockiness as he was unimpressed by their sheer attempt of intimidation. Vance stepped forward, sitting down at the desk with four members of the Department.

"I see you have my files." Vance said, seeing an open folder. "Well, did you read it? Or glance through it?'

"Mr. Harlan, we went over your works. Every bit of it."

"Every bit. Including the footnotes regarding the amount of energy needed to supply such a travel?"

The Officials sat still and Vance nodded slowly.

"I guess you did. Now I'm impressed."

"What we decided is that we cannot give you the funding for such a proposal."

"Why not? You read the file. You saw the details of this kind of mission. You know it's possible."

"Yes. We do." The second official said. "However, events prior to this mission have reverted our attentions elsewhere."

"Elsewhere? Like what the oceans?"

"This talk of alien life has gotten the public too far into our affairs and we, don't like that fact."

"But, come on. It's aliens. An opportunity to speak with intelligent life outside of our own planet."

"We hear you."

"But?' Vance said with a quick sigh of breath.

"We're invested in or current public affairs. The funding must go there."

"I don't agree with this."

"Doesn't matter if you do or do not." The third official said. "The decision has been made regardless of your work."

Vance wiped his face and slanted his head. He clapped his hands, startling the officials and jolting the guards. Vance looked around at he guards, seeing their firearms slightly raised. He waved them off with a laugh.

"Even they get startled."

"Thank you for your time with us, Mr. Harlan. You may go."

"I do however have one question to ask you. Just one."

"What is it?" The first official said.

"What is the true reason you have denied me funding for this project?"

The first official sighed before gazing over to the other three. The second official shook his head, staying silent. The third official fanned his hands in the air and didn't give an answer. The fourth official stared at Vance and turned to the first official.

Giving him a nod. Vance's eyes moved back and forth between the for officials.

"So, is he going to tell me or are you? I'm confused right now with all this staring and waving."

"I will speak it for you." The fourth official said.

"Good." Vance replied. "That's good. Now, what is it?"

"There was an incident that occurred over a month ago in Nevada."

"Nevada. Ok. I'm still not getting at what you're trying to tell me."

"An incident of forceful attacks took place at Area 51. One of our lieutenants went missing in the light of fire after the base was ambushed. He was unable to be found and is still missing."

"I see. But, with all due respect, what does a missing lieutenant have to do with my project's funding?"

"The cause of the attack were those intelligent beings you're so amazed by. They ambushed the base and attacked our men. Killed many and one of our best lieutenants is nowhere to be found. Now, do you understand why we cannot permit this project to go forward? Because those things you desire to meet, they want us all dead and this world theirs."

"Well, maybe they were antagonistic aliens. I mean all aliens cannot be enemies, sir. That's just not possible."

"Either way. This project is not going forward. You may leave us now, Mr. Harlan. Return to your other work. It's proven useful for our country and your life."

Vance stood up from the desk, grabbing his file. He still continued speaking with the officials, pleading they give him the funding. The officials continued to refuse until the guards stepped down from their post and surrounded Vance. Fully realizing his current predicament, Vance nodded and chuckled before taking his leave. Vance had returned to his home and from here, he set for to find a way to get his project going without the funding from the Department. Working nonstop for months while living in the outskirts of Phoenix, Arizona looking for an opportunity, Vance had come into communication with a much-wealthy foreign billionaire. The billionaire did not give Vance his name or location, only that he was interested in Vance's work and handed him the funding he needed. The billionaire's only request was for Vance to return to Earth once he had come into contact with extraterrestrials and that he should bring back with him physical evidence of their existence. Vance agreed to the commands and went ahead with the project. From there, a starship was built under the eyes of his colleagues and associates. Vance kept the project's workings to himself to avoid scrutiny and possible arrest from the government.

"Ah." Vance said, gazing at the starship. "She is finished."

The starship sat inside one of the hangars Vance had acquired from the military due to his previous works. Everything was in place for the travel and Vance had decided to wait until one clear night had come to make his launch. A week had passed and there was no clear sky due to the amount of clouds and precipitations of rainfall. Vance was annoyed by the weather's behavior. As if it was acting aggressive toward him, trying to get him to quit his project. Vance didn't quit and after a long day of rain, the night had come and the sky was clear. Vance had gathered all his gear and placed it inside the starship. The hangar had opened and the starship had launched into the sky. Vance was astonished at the speed of the ship and the stars around him. Several minutes had passed before Vance found himself in space, glancing out of the window looking down at Earth. Using a map he had placed inside the ship to navigate his goings. He went ahead and traveled. Passing through a stream of asteroids, a flash of light peaked through them, gaining Vance's attention. He moved toward through the meters toward the moving light. Once he came closer, the light flashed with such brightness that it caused the ship to jolt and from there, Vance could feel himself being pulled into the light and the ship with him. Vance kept his eyes shut from the blinding white-then-blue-then-red light. In a short spot of chance, Vance took a peek and saw the light was in fact a wormhole. A smile had formed on his face as he and the ship were sucked in and the light was gone. As if it was nowhere to be found. Like it was never in the stream of asteroids.

Within seconds, the ship was forced out of the wormhole with such speed, the ship had crashed onto a planet. Vance was calm, yet angry of his ship's damage. Exiting the damaged ship. Vance looked around, realizing he could breathe in the air. He looked down, seeing soil and grass. He grabbed the dirt and looked closer. It appeared to be no different than the soil on Earth.

"Shit!" Vance said. "Crashed back down to Earth."

While sighing in anger, the sound of a rushing wave crashed behind him. Vance had turned, looking at what he cold tell was a shoreline and the waves were crashing in with such force the ground had not flooded. Confused, he took a glance up to the sky and noticed it was a strange color. Not like the blue sky of Earth, but a very light greenish sky mixed with a layer of blue.

"What the hell?"

Vance had turned around to find himself quickly surrounded by beings that appeared to be hybrids. They had the upper bodies of animals and lower bodies of humans. They held what Vance could perceived to be guns toward him as he held his arms up. Somewhat shaking in fear. Not from the guns. One of the hybrids that appeared to be a Leopard-Man stepped forward, measuring Vance. He nodded.

"Take him back to the ship!"

"Ship?!" Vance said. "What ship?!"

CHAPTER 2: WELCOME ABOARD

Tossed onto a ship decorated with skulls of various creatures. Creatures unknown to Vance's knowledge, the ship took off across the waters as the crew passed him by, operating the ship's movement. Vance sat confused. Mainly confused by the living hybrids passing him by. Standing up, he wandered around the ship, attempting to ask questions concerning where he is. Turning around as the sea's waters rush against the ship, tilting it back and forth, Vance approached an somewhat middle-aged man dressed in Captain's garbs.

"Pardon me, but, where am I?"

"Where are you? My good sir, you aren't aware of your current circumstances?"

"What circumstances must I be aware of?"

"We found you on that small island. Looked to me, you must've crashed from the sea above us. We found you stranded out here. Brought you onboard to keep you alive. You do want to remain alive, don't you?"

"Well, yes I do. But, I'm not understanding. Where am I?"

"Where were you going?"

"I was going through a wormhole and I fell back down. I must be somewhere around the Pacific Islands. I have to be."

"Pacific Islands? What is that?"

Vance paused, looking at the Captain with uncertainty. He nodded while waving his hands, taking a gaze out toward the ocean.

"I'm still not understanding." The Captain said.

"We're on the Pacific Ocean, aren't we?"

"You're on the Sea of Aphro. The land around you is the Land of Aphro."

"Aphro?" Vance said. "What is Aphro?"

The Captain led Vance toward his study within the ship, passing by more hybrid creatures working. They enter the study with the first thing Vance noticed were the amount of scrolls laying on the shelves and the desk. The Captain approached his desk and opened a drawer, searching through, he grabbed a scroll and signaled Vance to approach the desk. Vance stepped forward as the Captain opened the scroll.

"What is this?" Vance asked.

"A map of this planet. Where we are right now is in the District of Aphro. Riding over the Seas of course."

"Planet? You said planet?"

"I did. Yes."

"Hold on. So, you're telling me, we're not on Earth?"

"Earth?" The Captain said confusingly. "What is Earth?"

"Earth. You know the third planet from the sun."

"Third planet? Third planet... Oh, you speak about Jarok. You're from Jarok?"

"Jarok? No. I'm from Earth."

"But, you said third from the sun."

"That is Earth."

"It is where you're from. Here, it's pronounced Jarok. Other words have been thrown out before. Depending on what planet you land on."

"So, if this is not Earth, then where am I?'

"Vanok."

"What is Vanok?"

"The second planet from the sun. second before Jarok and

second after Firoh."

"Firoh? Jarok? I'm not understanding these terms completely. You mean Earth and Mercury?"

"If that's what they're called wherever you're from?" The Captain replied. "So, you are from Jarok. Tell me, how are things there? We never receive news regarding that planet. Only the other ones around it."

Vance took a moment to catch his breath. Taking all of the information in slowly. If possible. He glanced down at the map, seeing the landmarks. What Vance noticed quickly was the amount of water upon Vanok and the mid-to-small sized islands surrounding two larger continents. He pointed at the continents with questions. What were they and who dwelled upon them. Asking the Captain concerning the two continents. The Captain chuckled, using a cane to point toward the continents.

"The one we're nearby, Aphro. Of course. The other is Vetor. Now, there is a difference between the two."

"What kind of difference?"

"Well, for starters, Aphro is a continent filled with rugged structures and a plethora of diverse creatures. That's where my hybrid pirates come in."

"A whole continent filled with beasts."

"Yes. Now, Vetor. It's a much different place. Surrounded by beautiful landmarks and cathedrals. From tall skyscrapers to temples to the Vanokian gods. Vetor is the home of the Kingdom of Vetoria."

"And have you ever been there? To this kingdom?"

The Captain laughed, taking a breath before walking over toward his shelf, where a bottle of rum sat. Grabbing the bottle and taking a drink.

"Never. My kind, meaning my line of work isn't seen as acceptable in such a place. The people of the kingdom perceive myself and those like me as subservient. Lesser living beings. The kingdom believes they're above all life on Vanok. Even their own children to an extent."

Vance remained quiet as the Captain took a moment of silence. He sighed and returned to drinking the rum as the ship rocked. Strangely enough, Vance felt the movement of the ship a bit strange. The ship rocked once more with the sound of a bang following. He stood up from his seat, looking around.

"Did you hear that?"

"Hear what?" The Captain asked.

"The explosion. Something's happening."

"Let's find out."

The two run out to the front, seeing the pirates clashing against another set of pirates as the opposing ship crashed into their own. From the other ship jumped over pirates of a different kind. Wearing worn-and-torn clothing with a particular circular insignia layered on their chest. Vance kept his distance as the Captain yelled for his pirates to assemble and fight against the others. Vance watched on as the swords clashed and the gunfire rung. In the distance on the other ship, Vance spotted a figure making themselves known. Looking closer, he saw the figure in full form.

"A woman?"

The woman stepped onboard the Captain's ship and fought against several of his hybrid pirates with a cutlass of her own. She took them down in seconds as she made her way toward the Captain. Vance sought to help, grabbing a sword on the floor and rushing toward the woman. Seeing him from the corner of her eye, she turned with speed clashing her cutlass against Vance's sword. She glared into his eyes and showed a slight grin.

"You're different." She uttered. "This is the ship."

The woman signaled her pirates to grab Vance and they tossed him onto the other ship as the Captain looked on fighting against the invaders. Making the move to assist Vance, he was slashed in the back by one of the pirates before the woman rallied her own to return to their ship. They moved with motion, returning to the ship and they escaped the area. The Captain stood up, sighing in pain went around to check on his pirates. Seeing some of them dead on the deck, he sighed bitterly.

"Her." He whispered to himself.

CHAPTER 3: CALYPSO

Vance had sat on the deck of the opposing ship, surrounded by the invading pirates. Their eyes eluded him. Glowing in many glares of color. From black, brown, green, blue, and red. The pirates snarled at Vance, attempting to terrify him. Yet, Vance kept his composure and faced them. The pirates from that point had paused themselves and moved over to the edges of the ship, making way for their captain to step forward. She walked with a vigorous stature as her eyes were set only on Vance. She approached him and looked down onto him. A grin had formed on her face.

"What's going on?" Vance asked. "Why did you take me?"

"Poor one. You aren't aware of the workings here. I can sense you're not from this world."

"Of course not. I come from Earth. As I was telling the Captain on the ship."

"You mean the Captain of those degenerate pirates?! Ha! Such company will poison you. Eventually killing you."

"Then, why take me from them? I was seeming to be doing just fine. Doing well for the most part since I crashed on this planet. What is all of this and where are you taking me?"

"Hold your temper and follow me."

The pirates escorted Vance behind the woman into her study. Looking similar to the Captain's own, yet detailed with colorful marbled walls and a stone-layered floor. Vance saw the floor and took a look back out to the deck, looking at its wooden bottom. He had questions and the woman only replied with the notion of her ship's design was possible due to her line of work. Vance wondered what work she spoke of as she sat down at her desk, covered with books and maps. Even a small emerald sat on the desk in the right corner. Like a pedestal of her achievements.

"Leave us." She told her pirates.

Exiting the study, Vance stood in the center of the room with the woman signaling him to sit down. He went and faced her. Sitting down and staring while admiring her exquisite interior design work. Vance gave a nod. Impressed by her choice of style. She waved it off like a small gesture of good fortune.

"You may be wondering why I took you from those hybrids and why you're here."

"I am wondering? What was the reason. How come you're different than your crew?"

"Because they've learned to respect me."

"I guess you were just a woman looking to do something others refused?"

"Refused is a slight word to use in my line of work. No, they did not refuse, yet, they didn't survive the pathways."

"Survive?"

"Most of the people on this planet strive to live. It is a necessary evil one must do in order to obtain food, water, and supplies to maintain their lives. The majority on this planet have even scraps to survive. To make amends to their gods and to keep their families safe. The some, they only seek to acquire whatever it is they need and they're content. So they shall be. But, the few. Oh, the few. The few do what they must to survive. Even if they have to slaughter, make war, or enter conflict with the others. In the end, the few have always won. Vanok is their world and not the other way around."

Vance nodded slowly, taking in her words.

"And you happened to be one of the few?"

"I am now. Before I was one of the majority. My mother and father did what they could to give me a proper childhood. However, war had fallen and my father went into battle. He survived the conflict, of course. But, his health declined due to the weapons used in the war. Chemicals that have transferred the sky above into the warping it appears today. Afterwards, my mother took care of me until I was able to take care of myself. I learned as I traveled the two continents. Searching for new ways of work and opportunity. The majority had always preached to me that marriage was in my future. That I would find a man who I would be suitable to match. Funny, after all the men I've encountered, none of them saw me as wife potential."

"I'm sorry to hear that." Vance said slowly.

"Don't be. It taught me something important. As I learned the true nature of this world, I became one of the Some. Learning new things and new ways to make things work. I tried to tell those I knew in my past abut these things and they refused. Saying, 'You can't live like that. It's too difficult to make such a path. The carving would be detrimental to one's own health.'. Crazy stuff they believe. Yet, that's what holds them down. Holds them back from increasing themselves. Elevating one's self is a sure way to make a move in this world."

"And what kind of carving did you make for yourself in this world?"

"First off, was military duty. I served in the Navy of the Kingdom of Vetoria. Fought countless battles on and off the seas. Most of my conflict was with the hybrids. We are taught in the forces the hybrids are responsible for more of the planet's dire circumstances. The increasing of the seas and the warping sky. All caused by their existence. The Navy's task was to eliminate any hybrids we encountered. And so we did."

"So, now you lead a group of pirates to do what exactly? Hold on. Is that why you ambushed the ship and took me?"

"Yes and no. Yes as in I ambushed the ship because they were hybrids. It's in my nature now. And no. I did not attack them simply to take you. Well, I didn't know you were onboard to start with. My intentions were simply elsewhere. That is until I saw you myself. From that point I had to take you."

"But why?"

"You're not a Vanokian. That much is true. Your essence oozes off your body. Your spirit's scent emits from you like a foreign soul."

"You know I'm not from this planet then."

"Certainly. What I want to know is why did you come here? What attracted you to Vanok in the first place?"

"First off, I didn't even know there was a Vanok to begin with. I was simply traveling through a wormhole and I ended up here. That is what happened."

"Truly?"

"Yes. Otherwise I would've had directions to go. I had no directions other than a wormhole."

"You said you're from Earth." The woman said, leaning in her chair. "Tell me, what is this Earth you speak of?"

"As I told the Captain of the Hybrids, Earth is the third planet from the sun. Second to Venus and first to Mars."

"I've never heard of Earth or Venus or Mars. They sound interesting though. That I'll give to you."

"I must be in a whole different solar system."

The woman reached down and picked up a map, she laid it out on the desk and slid it closer to Vance. He leaned over and looked. It was a map of a solar system. Yet not the one he is knowledgeable of. The planets on the map were bigger and the stars were brighter. Even it's sun was more of a darker fireball than the sun he knew.

"From what you're telling me, you most certainly are. Listen, this is what this system offers you. The first planet from the sun is what we like to call Firoh, a fiery planet. Its air will consume anything it touches. Second is Vanok, where we sit this day. A planet covered in much water and less land. Third is Jarok. A mysterious planet. We often wonder if there is life on it at all. Besides that, the tech capable of interstellar flight is kept in the secret chambers of the King of Vetoria. Fourth is what we call Arton, a planet covered in red dust. We speculate no life has been on that planet for millenniums. Fifth is Zutah, the planet of the Eye. Not sure what that means. Scholars here are still speculating. Sixth is Tharnog, surrounded with debris it gives off a bright light the father you're from it. You can slightly see it during the nights. Seven is Ocenia. Called that because it is known to be a planet of only water. No land."

"But, how are you certain of this? Of all of this?"

"Because of the scholars. They keep the records of the history of the system. The books have been around for ages."

Vance nodded, wiping the sweat from his forehead.

"This is a lot to take in."

"It has that affect on newcomers. But, don't you fret, there's still a lot more to learn."

"I see."

"Now, back to what I was saying. Oh, yeah. Now. The eighth planet is called Poston, somewhat similar to Oceania in appearance. However, instead of roaring waters, suffocating mists."

"I'm not certain as to how that works."

"You breath it in, you die. Simple as that."

Vance looked at the map again, seeing two remaining planets. The one after Poston was smaller and white as snow. The planet after was as dark as coal. the two planets seemed to mirror each other, according to Vance's understanding. The woman noticed his interest in the two planets as she smiled and tossing back her long wavy hair.

"Those two are enigmas of their own."

"And why is that?"

"The one before is called Hailon, a planet covered in dense snow. Often times, the scholars believe its pouring snow every second of a day. Can you imagine, nonstop snowfall for the rest of your days?"

"No I cannot. Where I live, snow is a rare occasion. Often appearances. But, rare."

"You're saying it doesn't snow on Earth?"

"No. It snows. Yes. But, not everywhere gets it. Only portions receive it. If you understand what I'm trying to say."

"I hear you."

"Does it snow here? In these waters?"

"Several times during the Sapphire Cycle. But, that's a whole 'nother tale."

"And what of the last planet? It looks a bit eerie."

"Because it is. We call that one simply Abyssian."

"Abyssian?" Vance said. "Like the abyss?"

"Why else name it after."

The woman sighed as she glanced over to a clock which sat against the ship walls. Seeing the time, she stood up and called for her pirates to return. Entering the study, they surround Vance and hold him up as he begins asking more questions concerning his fate. The woman laughed as she approached him closely.

"At least tell me what you want from me?"

"Oh. I want nothing from you. But, I know someone who will."

"I'm not understanding."

"We're on our way to the Kingdom of Vetoria. The King will like to have a word with you."

"The King?" Vance asked. "Why me?"

"Because you're the first being to come from another planet in ages. Such an event is one the King would not like to miss."

"Hold on. How does he know I'm here?"

"We have our ways of contact. Remember me saying something about tech earlier. It works in many ways. Ways the Majority will never come to understand and the Some refuse to use in order to advance themselves."

The woman commanded the pirates to take Vance to the guest room on the ship. Dragging him down the hallway, they opened the door and tossed Vance inside. Shutting the door before he could make a turn-around. Vance looked at the room, seeing a bed, a dining table, and a shelf of books. He looked over toward the shelf, looking at the books' spines, reading the titles. They were a mystery to him. All spoke about constellations and mysticism. Something Vance is not of interest in. While he were searching through, a knock came from the door, startling him. He stood up from his knees and called out tot eh visitor. The door had opened and it was the woman. Closing the door behind her as Vance stood confused.

"Why are you putting me in here?"

"To give you some comfort before you meet the King."

"None of this is making sense."

"I can't treat you like a slave and bring you to the King. He'll see the way you were treated and make a conclusion from that point. He has ways which are peculiar to foreigners."

Vance nodded while sitting down at the dining table. The woman looked and nodded. Something came to her attention. She called her hands, startling Vance as she laughed. He shook his head, trying to keep his composure and mental state. This is a day he never expected to live. But, here he is.

"Very well. I'll have some food brought to you and you can take a moment to rest before you meet the King."

"Well, thank you for your sudden hospitality. Could've doe this earlier and I may have taken you differently."

"The day is not over and I am not easy to comprehend. Nor are my motives."

The woman turned to exit the room, but Vance called out to her. Catching himself before even thinking of what to say next. She stood still, waiting for Vance to speak. He nodded and had a thought. A simple one.

"You never told me your name? That is if you have one."

"My name." she said. "You want to know my name?"

"I would like to. Otherwise, I would have to refer to you as the woman who took me from the ship or the Invader."

"As much as I would prefer those two, I'll tell you my name. although, I must warn you. Not even my crew knows of my name and for your sake, I would like to keep it that way."

"Wait, how do they not your name? so, they simply call you Captain?"

"Captain is enough for them to know who I am and my worth."

Vance nodded in agreement. He understood her intentions for once. The woman took a breath before uttering another word. Something which took Vance off his guard. Seeing a slightly vulnerable state from the woman who invaded another's ship and fought off the hybrids before taking him.

"Calypso is my name."

"Calypso." Vance said. "Sounds, a little frightening."

"As it should be."

Calypso turned and left the room, leaving Vance in a frozen state of worry and insight. Vance sighed as he could hear the waves moving across the seas.

CHAPTER 4: THE KINGDOM OF VETORIA

Vance woke up to the waves and the running sounds of the pirates heading toward the deck. Getting himself up, he rushed outside the room and followed the pirates, leading him to the deck where Calypso stood. She looked out to her crew and saw Vance in the distance. She smirked with a nod. Turning around, she faced the direction and toward them was the Kingdom of Vetoria. She held up her hands, shouting a war cry in Vanokian dialect to which all the pirates rallied with her while Vance stood confused. Calypso approached Vance as he began ask her of the war cry.

"I said, Hail Vetoria. Hail to the gods."

"Oh." Vance replied. "I thought it was something of the likes of taking over the city."

"I couldn't do that to the King. However, I could if I chose to."

The ship made its way toward the landing deck as the pirates tossed over the anchor. Jumping off the ship, Calypso kept Vance close to her in avoiding the Vetorians who saw them arrive, staring at them like guard dogs protecting their home. Vance stared at them, even to the degree of Calypso warning him not to cause a scene. The Vetorian people were dressed modestly. The men wore slacks and long-sleeve robes in which reminded Vance of the Ancient Greek imagery. The women were fully dressed from head to toe decked in dresses and head coverings. Even to Vance's surprise, he happened to notice the women did not wear any makeup. He rubbed his eyes looking closer as he passed them by. Calypso noticed his interest and tugged him.

"What are you doing?"

"They're not wearing makeup."

"Makeup?" Calypso said. "What is makeup?"

"The women I knew, they would design their faces. Making them look more appealing."

Calypso scoffed.

"Is that what they do on Jarok? They paint their faces like the jesters of the court?"

"When you put it that way, maybe." Vance shrugged.

The overall landscape of Vetoria was one of a beautifully appearance. Attractive to the yes were its polished grounds and structures. Merchants passed them by on marble-like wagons and carriages. Even the animals passing by were of a different breed. Vance thought them to be cows, but given a much closer examination he spotted black dots across the back of the animals. From the carved designs of their gods scattered around and nearby the palace to the monuments inscribed concerning Vetorian laws and guidelines.

They approached the entry point to the Vetorian Palace. The monumental structure detailed in much sapphire and built with a light blue stone. The paint covered across the palace was nearly transparent to the waters which roared nearby. Vance also realized the air was different than the island of Aphro, much smoother and the sky was much clearer. Clear to the point, Vance could see the stars peeking through the thin clouds. The palace doors opened with two guards standing by. Wielding tridents in their right hands. The guards nodded toward Calypso and her two close pirate guards as they gave Vance a stare. A look of uncertainty as Vance nodded to them. They did not respond. Entering the throne room, Calypso looked ahead, seeing the King sitting. She stopped herself and turned to Vance as he noticed the King. The King himself wore the diverse garb of land and sea. From the hides of the beasts of the land to the teeth and scales from the creatures of the seas. However, his crown was made of pure sapphire and his staff was made of pure emerald. Yet, there was gold layered upon his throne. Vance saw it and only shook his head. He has never seen so much sapphire, emerald, or even gold in his life. It was all just a dream to him.

"Before we enter, do what I say."

"Like what? Bow before him and don't give eye contact?"

"Exactly. You're smarter than you look, Jarokian."

Walking into the throne room, a room decorated with sapphire floors and ceilings. Painting layered across the walls detail a history of the planet. Vance stared at them. Seeing everything from pirates at war with royal navies, marriages, and even monsters from the seas clashing with enlightened beings coming down from the sky. The King saw them and smiled. waving toward Calypso as he stood up and hugged her. He greeted the two pirate guards and paused, looking at Vance. His eyes slanted over toward calypso with question. She nodded with a smile.

"I can explain this man's unknown arrival."

"Do explain."

The King sat down as Calypso began to explain Vance's reasoning for standing in his throne room. Calypso introduced Vance to the King, King Kharan. Vance waved to no reply from Kharan. Calypso told the king of Vance's possible value to his kingdom and what he can do in order to achieve a place in the Vetorian landscape. Calypso even pointed out the details of Vance's arrival from another planet. Kharan asked what planet did Vance originate from and Vance held his hand up to their surprise.

"Earth. I come from Earth."

"What is Earth?" Kharan asked Calypso. "I've never heard of this Earth before?"

"He speaks of Jarok, my King." Calypso answered. "This man is a native to Jarok. He came here by ship."

"Jarok. You came from the planet after us?"

"I did, King Kharan. Where I'm from, we call it Earth. It's simple."

"So it may be. Tell me, why come here? Why not traverse the stars and reach a planet filled with a much greater life than exists here? A planet with much land and sea for everyone to share?"

"To be honest, I wasn't even sure where I was headed. I traveled and discovered a wormhole and from there I arrived here. Or crashed here. However you perceive the arrival."

"And what do you intend to do from this point forward?"

"I would like to return home eventually. To tell everyone I know about this place."

"And tell them why? To entice some to war. If you could travel here through a one-way tunnel, then so could they. War is not what we need in this day and hour. We already have enough conflicts with the hybrids that roam the lands and scavenge the seas. From what I can sense, you had a confrontation with them."

"Not as much as a confrontation. More like a meeting without knowing."

"Calypso, my dear. Where did you find this man?"

"I found him on the ship of the Captain of the Hybrids."

"He was with them?" Kharan said, standing up from his seat. "And you brought him here?"

"It's not like that, my King."

"Then how is it?"

"I attacked their ship as you commanded all of us to do. While ambushing, I discovered Vance on the ship. To me, he appeared to be a slave to the Captain. He wasn't around the others nor did he act like them. His countenance told me he was of potential and that is why he's standing here before you."

Kharan sat back down and scratched his beard. Giving both Vance and Calypso eyes of questioning. Calypso hung her head while Vance looked around at the throne room's design. Taking another look at the paintings and smiled.

"Who designed those?"

"An artist who spent much time in Vetoria. He still does paintings for us this day."

"That's cool. Can I meet him?"

"No."

"Fair enough."

Kharan sighed, looking toward Calypso and Vance.

"I have a proposition for you. The both of you actually."

"I'm all ears." Vance said.

"What is it, my King?"

"I will see what this Jarokian can do. I will test his might, his skill, his mentality, and lastly, his spirit. I want to see if the people of Jarok are as, stable as the legends tell them to be."

"Wait. You said legends."

"I did."

"You mean you're aware on life on Earth. I mean Jarok?"

"I do. Many of the scrolls kept in the achieves chamber by my scholar have indicated the people of Jarok are somewhat above us. In skill, technology, and spirituality."

"I wouldn't put us up to that kind of stature. But, I see your concerns."

"But, since you're from Jarok. Are the people as the legends say or are they less?"

"It's complicated to say the least. Some are and some aren't."

"Depends on where one goes, doesn't it?" Kharan asked.

"It does."

"Hmm. Well then, time will reveal all things. This man seems to have some potential indeed, Calypso."

"He will not prove you wrong, my King. I am positive he has the skills capable of cleansing this planet of the hybrids just as you desire."

"We shall see once the tests are complete. Maybe your words prove right about this man, Calypso. However, maybe you're wrong. But in the end, it is this man who will provide us all with the answer."

While they spoke, the sound of a door opening creaked behind Kharan. He stood up and looked back, seeing a young woman entering the throne room. Kharan smiled as Calypso bowed and Vance stood still. Staring at the young woman. Dressed in red apparel from her neck down. She wore golden rings on her fingers and layered gold laced within her dress. She even had a golden tiara and necklace to match.

"Vance Harlan of Jarok, allow me to introduce to you my daughter, Serilda. She has been praying for a warrior to arrive to aid her father in his conquest of ridding this planet of the hybrids. Perhaps, you are that warrior. Perhaps, my daughter's prayers have been answered by the gods."

Vance nodded to Serilda and she nodded back. Yet, their eyes had locked with one another and immediately Vance was pulled into a void. A void unseen by anyone else in the throne room. Vance moved throughout the void, leaning he was outside of his body as he turned around seeing himself, Calypso, Serilda, and Kharan standing in the throne room.

"What is going on?"

"I have prayed for you to come." A voice said within the void.

"Prayed for me? I'm not understanding what you ask of me."

"You can be the light to Vanok. The pathway to a new world. A world where Vetorians and hybrids can live as one. As one people."

"Listen, I'm just a man. I don't fight wars for conquest that are beyond my comprehension. This isn't even my home."

"But, you are here for a reason. A reason which has been chosen well by the gods."

"I don't know these gods."

"In time, you will come to know. Everyone on Vanok does eventually. Now wake up."

Within seconds, Vance awoke to find himself standing in the same place and his eyes were still locked on Serilda. However, when Vance came to the understanding of the sudden void, Serilda gave him a smirk before she took her leave. Kharan stepped forward toward Vance, placing his hand on his shoulders. Kharan turned to Calypso.

"Calypso, I will take him from here. I'm sure there are a plenty things you have to attend to."

"Yes, my king. I do have one question. If I may ask."

"Speak."

"The Captain of the Hybrids will soon be coming for Vance Harlan. The sense in the air tells me he'll be making his way here to find him."

"And you want me to grant you permission to face him head-on?"

"If you would like him out of your hairs, then yes."

Kharan nodded with a grin.

"Good. Good. Go and cleanse our waters of the hybrid filth. Return to me when the task is complete. A reward will be waiting for you when you arrive."

"I will do as you command."

"Vance Harlan of Jarok. My guards will bring you to one of our luxurious rooms. You will stay here for the night as your tests will begin on the morrow. Best to rest yourself before the trails of your life begin."

Calypso bowed before she made her leave as the Vetorian guards escorted Vance to one of the guest rooms of the palace. Arriving at the room, Vance immediately noticed the layout of the room. Reminding him of the wealthy places to stay on Earth. From a nice balcony over looking the city and the sea to the decorated furniture. Even the air was cleaner than the outside. The guards left Vance as he sat down gazing out toward the city, hearing the voices of the people mixed with the rushing waters of the sea.

Elsewhere on the seas, the Captain of the Hybrids sat down in his study, overlooking the map with a marking directed onto the Kingdom of Vetoria. From the study doors entered one of the hybrids. A being which looked to be a leopard mixed with a human. The leopard portion on the upper body and the human portion on the lower.

"Boss, we've received word from the others."

"What is this word?"

"They've said to have seen the foreigner. The one who fell from the sky."

"Have they? And where did they see him?"

"Vetorian sir. He was escorted by Calypso toward the palace."

The Captain raised his head from the map. Rolling up the map and setting it aside. He laid back in his chair as he thought to himself. He raised himself up back to the desk and opened the map again, this time staring at the red markings over Vetoria.

"So, she means to make him a tool of war for Kharan, huh. Well then, I guess they won't be expecting us when we arrive. They want war. Let's give them a war."

CHAPTER 5: A TEST OF FORTITUDE AND KNOWLEDGE

Vance arose to the sound of the waters as he gazed outside, seeing the Vetorian people going about their day as they did before. Taking in the scenery, a knock thundered from the door. Vance turned around, speaking for the visitor to enter. The door opened as Kharan himself entered the room. Vance saw him and nodded his head in reverence.

"I take it you received a well night's rest?"

"I did. One I haven't had in a long time."

"Very well. That is good to hear. Because you will require all the energy you can muster this day. For it will be a challenging one."

"What kind of trials are set for me today?"

"A variety of sorts. First, prepare yourself. Eat well and my guards will bring you to the arena for the first trial."

"Arena?" Vance paused. "Like a fighting arena?"

"Are there any others?"

"I see."

"You will once you arrive. Take this time, Vance Harlan of Jarok. Take it well."

Kharan exited the room, leaving Vance to take the moment to prepare himself. Vance had sighed, gazing back out to the open area of the city. From there, Vance knelt down near the bed and began to pray. He prayed for protection against any adversary which may be awaiting him at the arena. Afterwards, Vance ate the breakfast which was delivered to him immediately after his prayer. Once he was finished, a knock came from the door. Vance went and opened it, seeing two guards. He nodded and exited the room. Walking with them down the hall and followed them toward the arena. The arena itself was over thirty stories and there was no audience sitting in attendance, just yet. Standing in the middle of the arena was Kharan as he applauded Vance's arrival.

"You have come. Good. Good. Now, are you ready to hear what is being presented to you?"

"Ready as I'll ever be."

"Then let us begin!"

The arena doors shut and around Vance were several men dressed in light blue robes. Their faces shrouded by their hoods. In their hands were scrolls, worn and torn. The men opened the scrolls and laid them on the table which sat before Vance. Eight scrolls in total. Kharan commanded for Vance to approach the table and read the first one. Vance went and read it. Strangely to him, the scrolls were written in Vanokian, but he was able to read them as if they were English.

"What is this?"

"The first test of knowledge." Kharan answered. "To test your mind and your history."

Vance read the scroll in detail. Gaining the understanding he needed to comprehend this first test. Kharan kept his sights on Vance, seeing his mannerisms and facial changes.

"What does it say?" Kharan asked.

"It asks me to describe the difference between your world and mine."

"Then, describe it."

"What is there to describe. From what I've seen since my time on this planet, their behaviors and the appearances of the people are no different than the ones back on Earth. In a creepy way, they're both very similar."

Kharan nodded. He waved his hand toward the hooded one, who rolled up the first scroll and stood aside. Vance turned toward the second scroll and read it. Kharan asked Vance to speak what it says.

"This one asks of me to detail the differences between the skies between your world and mine."

"Tell us, what are those differences?"

"For starters, Earth's sky is not contaminated by the celestial storms I see above us."

"Then what is it contaminated by?"

"A variety of things. Matters to discuss in a greater detail which would take up my time on this test."

"I see." Kharan noted.

The second hooded one rolled up the scroll and stood aside as Vance approached the third scroll.

"This one speaks of the difference between the arts of war."

"Arts of war." Kharan said. "This will prove useful. Tell us, what are the differences?"

"The difference is there are no differences." Vance answered. "War is the same wherever you go. No matter the species which dwells upon the planet."

"By such words, you confirm that war is eternal?"

"War is eternal. The struggle keeps civilizations going until the end of all things."

"Noted."

The scroll was rolled up and Vance approached the fourth. The fourth one detailed the similarities between the animals on Earth compared to Vanok. Kharan asked Vance to give the answer and Vance only sighed.

"So far, I've never encountered any hybrids until I came here."

"Interesting." Kharan replied. "You mean to tell me you've never seen any hybrids back on your planet?"

"None. I'm not saying they don't exist there. But, I've never encountered one."

"Good to hear. At least your world doesn't have to deal with the suffrage of those savage creatures. Seeking to destroy all you hold dear. Pillaging wherever they go. Such filth."

The fifth scroll was read and Vance took in the words. The words enticed him slightly as they pertained to the government rulings between both worlds. Kharan asked Vance to answer once more and Vance only replied by stating the governments between the two planets are not hat different. Pertaining to which country one visits to the individual in charge. Kharan nodded with intrigue. The sixth scroll was next to be read and upon the sixth scroll were two drawings. One of a man. Another of a woman. Kharan asked for Vance to give an answer to the question of the drawings. Vance looked at the drawings carefully.

"Without them both, the planet would be without those of dominion. It is the nature of the balance."

"Nature of the balance." Kharan said. "Interesting choice of wordplay. Next."

The seventh scroll was approached by Vance and detailed the societal order of both worlds. Vance quickly answered by saying the roles of man, woman, and child must remain in constant flow unless they deem the civilization itself to collapse and eventually end all that remains. Kharan took this words carefully, as it reminded him of how he became king. Through a much similar circumstance. The last scroll was approached and Vance stood still, taking in the question. Kharan stood boldly against the wall as Vance read the scroll.

"What does it say?" Kharan asked.

"It asks the question of honor between the two worlds. Honor is a must in all worlds. Without it, one will never see the days ahead. Only a quick and painful death awaits those who dishonor for a sport cause."

"Good words. Good words."

Kharan waved for the scrolls and the table to be removed from the arena floor. The scholars disappeared into the shadows circling them. Vance stood still as he began to hear the sound of doors opening and he gazed up to the seats, beginning to see the civilians enter the arena. Vance turned to Kharan, asking him what was about to happen. Kharan chuckled.

"Your next test. Combat."

"Combat?" Vance said. "Like right now?"

"Good place as any. Besides, you seem like a capable warrior who would defend himself if the cause came about. Now, the cause has arrived."

The guards entered the arena, tossing a rapier to Vance. He caught it and stared at the blade. Kharan walked toward him and handed him a firearm. Vance looked at the firearm and noticed there was something different.

"What kind of gun is this?"

"One you can only find within the walls of this palace. It will be of good use in your fights."

"But, how does it work?"

"You mean to tell me your kind don't have such weapons back on Jarok?"

"Oh no. we do. We have a lot of them. All different shapes and sizes. But, I'm just curious as to how this one works."

'You see the trigger?"

"Yes."

"Then you know how it works."

The crowds gathered within the arena and cheered as Vance looked up toward them. The doors in front of Vance on the other end of the arena had opened and out of them walked out three men. Two were guards of the palace while the third one appeared to be a pirate. One of Calypso's Vance had thought to himself. Kharan commanded the battle to begin and the three opponents rushed toward Vance. Hesitant to make an attack, Vance deflected the swords of the guards and the pirate. The guards moved with such speed that Vance had to double his efforts to keep up with their attacks. The pirate stood back and scoffed at Vance's defensive skills while making an attack in between the guards' own. Vance swiped the blade, knocking one of the javelins out of the guard's hand before shoving him to the ground to the audience's excitement. Te second Guard went to make a strike, Vance dodged the attack and used the gun to blast a hole through the guard's chest. Vance caught himself as he looked at the firearm, recognizing it was an energy gun as it fired a bright blue beam through the guard's chest as if it was nothing. The pirate stood still, looking down at the guard's body and made a run for it. Vance sighed as he waved to the audience and their cheers calmed him. Kharan nodded and approached Vance from his seat.

"Excellent work. You have done well."

"I hope this is over with. I'm not sure I can kill another. That was an accident."

"An accident or a gesture of self-defense? If you had not fired the shot, they would've killed you."

Vance knew this and took it well. Kharan nodded and waved toward the door. The doors had opened and this time only one figure emerged from the shadows. Vance saw the figure, seeing it was a warrior clothed in greenish armor made from the scales of the sea creatures and in his hands he held a trident made of horns.

"You do however have one more battle." Kharan said. "Defeat him and you will enter the third and final portion of this test."

The audience roared as the gladiator entered the arena. Vance stood firm as his right hand was gripped onto the hilt of the rapier and his left hand was steady with the energy gun. The gladiator screamed to the audience's cheer as he ran toward Vance with the trident head-on. Vance moved out of the trident's path, slashing the blade across the gladiator's back. The blade impacted the armor, shattering small fragments of the scales. The gladiator paused and stared.

"It's a fight." Vance said. "What else am I supposed to do?"

The gladiator screamed, slamming the trident to the ground in front of Vance. He stepped back as the gladiator went for a punch, hitting Vance across his jaw as he pushed him to the ground. Vance looked around and fired a shot from the energy gun to the gladiator's chest. The armor shattered, but the beam did not pass through. Vance was surprised.

"You thought a beam could take me out?!" The gladiator yelled. "Do you know who I am?!"

"I'm afraid I don't." Vance replied. "Who are you supposed to be?"

"You fool! I am Batrion the Destroyer! This day, you will learn why I've earned it."

"I'm not so sure I will."

Batrion went fro another strike with the trident and Vance fired a shot at Batrion's hand. Dropping the trident from the blast, he looked at his hand. Seeing the shredded scales and feeling the burning over his skin. Vance grinned.

"I'm learning."

Batrion went for a punch and Vance dodged the attack, instead swiping the blade atop Batrion's hand, cutting it off. Batrion yelled as he fell to his knees, holding his severed wrist as hi hand laid on the floor to the audience's surprise. Vance sighed.

"Please yield."

Batrion glared into Vance's eyes, going for another attack with Vance only hitting him in the head with the energy gun. Batrion collapsed to the ground as the audience cheered Vance's victory. Kharan applauded as he stood up and granted Vance the winner of the day's battle. The audience began to leave as Kharan stood still with the hooded figures making their return into the arena. Batrion himself was carried out by the guards and his hand was taken as well. The hooded figures surrounded both Kharan and Vance as Kharan began to lay out the final portion of the test. The third and final portion pertaining to spirituality.

"Spirituality?" Vance asked. "Like what about it?"

"We want to know. I want to know. What do you believe in? Are there any gods back on your world the people worship? How many do they worship?"

"Well, it all depends on where one travels."

"I see. So, in your area of living, how many gods to they serve?"

"Depends on who you ask. It's a mixed-multitude in the country I live in."

"So, you mean to tell me, there can be one who worships one god while the other can worship a plethora of gods and they live on the same field?"

"Yes. That's what it's like. Unless you buy out the land for yourself and those of your like-mindedness."

Kharan nodded.

"Interesting. Now, I must ask you this question and this one will ensure your future upon this planet and within my kingdom."

"I'm listening."

"How many gods do you serve?"

"Honestly. I serve one."

"One. You serve one god?"

"Yes I do."

"And those you've met on your travels back on your world? Others you've shared conversations with? How many gods have they claimed to serve?"

"Some several. Many a lot. Few only serve one god."

"Such an enigma back on your world. Do you not know that where there's more gods, the better?"

"I'm not sure that confirms the clarification of worship."

"And why do you say that?"

"Because, where I'm from and how I was raised. There was only one god. He created everything and everyone."

"Everything and everyone on your world?"

"No, your Majesty. He created all things. Even this world we stand on today. He created even you."

The scholars lifted up their heads, staring at Vance with hatred searing in their eyes. Vance caught them by the feeling of an unsettling energy moving around the arena. Kharan stood still, calmly taking in Vance's words.

"He is a destroyer." One scholar spoke.

"He will destroy all you have built!" A second scholar spoke.

"Dispose of him, my King." The third scholar spoke.

"He is a blasphemer to the gods!" The fourth scholar spoke.

"Death and fire will rain down over all of Vanok if he remains!" The fifth scholar spoke.

The following three scholar spoke their own minds as the first five continued to repeat their statements. Kharan shook his head and grabbed his staff, slamming it into the floor, causing a crack to form as the sound of a shockwave echoed through the arena field.

"Silence yourselves!" Kharan yelled. "I will deal with him in matters of my own making."

The scholars hung their heads and stepped back three steps. Kharan approached Vance, looking him in the eyes. He nodded.

"Very well. I see you stand by your belief. That is something I highly respect in any individual. For one who stands for their beliefs is one I would align myself with for any cause."

Vance nodded in respect to Kharan's honor. Kharan allowed Vance to return to his room as the test were complete. Vance had passed. The guards entered and brought Vance back to his room while the scholars continued to speak against him. Kharan heeded their words and commanded for them to remain silent. One scholar refused and proclaimed that the gods of Vanok would strike down Kharan if he not rid the kingdom of Vance. Kharan took his staff and smashed it across the scholar's head and beat him to death in front of the others. The remaining seven stood silent as Kharan commanded for his guards to take the scholar's body and toss it into the seas.

"What happens to Vance will be of my choice. My decision. Not the gods." Kharan proclaimed as he left the arena.

CHAPTER 6: PIRATES OF VANOK

The Captain of the Hybrids and his crew rode across the roaring seas, following the trail on the map. The Captain kept his gaze on the surroundings. Seeing nothing but water in his sights. Up ahead, one of the hybrids ran forward with binoculars, handing them to the Captain.

"Ahead, sir!"

The Captain looked on and saw Calypso's ship up ahead. He knew she was coming for him and he grinned. Looking further behind her, he could see land. He screamed toward his crew they have arrived on the continent of Vetor. The crew cheered as they prepared themselves for battle. Over on the other ship, Calypso looked out toward them with her crew ready as their swords were drawn.

"He continues to act as if he will survive the journey." Calypso said. "Well, he will realize his end is nigh by the sharpness of my blade."

The two ships reached one another as the battle began with the hybrids clashing with the pirates. This time, the hybrids allowed thee animalistic urges to consume them, in so much as slaughtering Calypso's pirates with a certain ease. Calypso herself was not bothered by their animal rages as she sliced her way through them to get to the Captain. She walked on the deck, killing hybrids as she saw the Captain waiting for her with his sword drawn and a smile on his face.

"You think this is funny?!"

"I do. I have a dark sense of humor."

Calypso and the Captain's blades clashed with the sound of thunder above them. They locked eyes as the ongoing battles continued around them.

"Where did you take the foreigner?"

"None of your concern."

"It is of my concern. I was the one who found him first!"

"You would've wasted his potential! His skill!"

"I would've?! You took him to your king, didn't you?!"

The Captain swiped the sword as Calypso deflected the blade with her own. The two circled one another while taking out one from the other's crew. Their eyes still locked onto each other as rain began to pour down upon them. The Captain laughed, taking in the scenery.

"The Jarokian will prove a useful ally to the King in ridding this planet of your crew's kind. Such nature cannot allow to continue."

"Who gave you the right to determine who lives and who dies?! Your King?!"

Calypso nodded.

"It's my job."

"Kill me and my crew here and now, and maybe we'll see if it's your job."

Calypso screamed as she rushed against the Captain with her sword. The two battled on the deck in the midst of their crews. The Captain laughed continually as Calypso screamed like a siren. The blades clashed and clashed as sparks flew from them. Calypso twirled the blade and kicked the Captain in the abdomen as he fell. Rushing over to impale him, one of the hybrids jumped onto Calypso's back, biting her in the shoulder. She screamed as she plunged the blade into the hybrid's chest. The Captain arose and fought back against Calypso. More hybrids went to intervene, only to be killed by Calypso's blade. The captain kept fighting as several of Calypso's pirates moved in to attack him. Only for his hybrids ambush them by biting their necks or impaling them with their tails.

"You cannot win." Calypso said. "You have no right."

"Again, who gave you the right to determine who wins and who loses? Oh, that's right. Your job."

Calypso went to strike the Captain again, yet, a large lightning bolt crashed into the waters. Startling everyone, even the Captain as he made his move toward the wheel of the ship. Calypso looked around, seeing everyone returning to their own ships. Even her crew was afraid.

"Where are you going?!" This battle is not over!"

"We must go, my lady!" One of her pirates said. "The gods, they're angry at us all. We're in danger if we stay out here!"

"You'll be in danger if you allow those savages to live!"

She stood over the edge of the hybrid's ship against her own. Calypso turned around as the Captain dropkicked her back onto her ship as his ship made their escape. Standing up in haste, she looked out seeing the hybrids' ship heading towards Vetor. Screaming in anger, she turned her attention toward her crew. Yelling for them to fight back against the hybrids. However, some refused stating the lightning bolt was a sign of a truce between the two forces. Believing the gods have called off the ongoing war. Calypso scoffed as she dug her blade into several of their chests. She looked at the remaining members of her crew.

"If you are not with me, then you are not with your King!"

The crew stared at her with fear. Uncertain for their lives as they saw her take out several of their own crew members. She walked in front of them, wielding the blood-soaked sword in their faces. The blood brought forth another essence of fear upon them. For they were more afraid of Calypso now than before.

"Make your choice now. Are you with me? Are you with the

King? Or are you with those savages?"

The crew yelled they were with her and the king. Calypso nodded as she commanded tem to toss the dead bodies over into the seas. Obeying her word, once the bodies fell into the waters, a massive sea creature arose, covered in dark emerald-like scales and its eyes were as bright as the sun. The beast gazed around the waters, seeing the bodies and took them deep into the seas with its mouth. The crew saw it and fell for fear as Calypso grinned, seeing it as a sign of their coming victory.

CHAPTER 7: A WAY HOME?

Vance walked through the palace after being given permission by Kharan. He was astounded by the architecture. By walking through the corridors, he was able to see more of the interior. Along his walk, he discovered more paintings across the walls. Only these walls depicted a great war between the hybrids and the royals. One of the figures in the painting was Kharan himself wielding a glowing trident made of sapphire. The trident was struck by lightning as he was clashing against a hybrid beast of man, lion, and serpent. Continuing his walk, Vance ran into Serilda, startling her and himself.

"Wasn't expecting to see you here." Vance said. "Especially during this time of night."

"I am the Princess. Therefore, I have permission to gad abroad."

"So I can see."

"It appears you have completed my father's tests."

"I did. And not to my liking. Although, his tests were a bit strange for me. Not that I am a fighter by any means. The knowledge tests with the scrolls was easy for me to overcome. The combat however, that was a challenge."

"And the spiritual test? Was that as challenging as well?"

"It was easy. Tough but easy."

"Explain to me how it was tough? And why?"

"Because, I don't speak much on my beliefs. Personality, I

would prefer to keep them t myself. To avoid conflict."

"That's funny."

"How so?"

"Because we're taught to speak highly of our beliefs. It is those in which make us who we are. The things we do and the words we speak rely solely on the beliefs we share. If it were not for them, we would be vagabonds in the end. Heretics to a fallen cause."

Vance held his composure. He was amazed by the speech of a princess. Much less one who appeared physically to be so intelligent. Vance applauded her words of wisdom.

"You speak well. For someone like yourself."

"And they don't have women like me back on your world?"

"Women like you are a dying breed where I'm from. Although, there are a few every now and then. Scattered like the sands of the sea."

"Touching."

"It can't be all that bad." Vance said. "Seeing as how you're who you are. Your father must've done something well."

"He takes care of me and his people. It is his duty as king and as a father."

"Where is your mother?"

"She went off on some diplomatic duties to the west. The Kingdom of Nabel needed her guidance toward their concern regarding their women. My mother is skilled in setting places straight. To keep the balance in play."

"That's something worth knowing."

"I could tell you sense my father's rulings a bit harsh."

"In a sense. The ways he views the hybrids is something unnecessary. The hybrids only want to live in peace. They do not seek to fight."

"And how do you know this? Last I heard, you were aboard their ship. Possibly taken captive."

"No. I wasn't taken captive. They saved me."

"Saved you? From what?"

"My ship crashed. I was stranded on an island and they arrived. Brought me in and treated me well. As best they could before they were attacked by Calypso and her crew."

"Ah, Calypso." Serilda said. "I'm surprised she still is seen in good spirits toward my father."

"Calypso told me she does well for your father's kingdom. She despises the hybrids just as much as he does."

"That much is certain. However, Calypso sees much more in this field of war than slaughtering any hybrids she comes across. She wants a place to rule."

"How are you aware of this?"

"Because I've been in council meetings before. Where she would be welcomed. Her words always spoke of some kind of rule. Whether it was an island to call her own or a kingdom to dwell. Ruler-ship is something is craves deeply and the killing of hybrids will not cease that desire."

"I see why she's the way she is."

"Anyhow, why are you walking through the halls of the palace?"

"Just taking a gander of things. I saw the painting in the throne room when I first arrived. Didn't know there were many more scattered throughout the place."

"You should check the library. There's much in there to grab your attention."

"There's a library here?"

"Of course. I will take you to it."

From there, Vance followed Serilda through several sets of corridors, passing by the guards who stood like statues. Entering the western portion of the palace, Serilda opened the large double-doors which appeared to be made of wood layered with coral. Within the room was the library. Nearly three floors filled with scrolls and maps. Scattered in the library were small statuettes of ships pertaining to Kharan's Navy and the Navy before his rule. Vance stood at the entrance, shaking his head in wonder.

"Endless amounts of scrolls."

"Indeed." Serilda chuckled. "Besides, only those permitted to the palace can step foot in this place."

"You mean the people outside have no entry into this library? For what cause?"

"It's a royal decree. The people have the Library of Vetoria to themselves within the city."

"But, what's the difference between them? One gets standard information while the other gains a little extra notes."

"Some matters of this continent's history must be protected by the royals. It is the decree of the ancients. Their rule and my father continues it to this day."

Vance walked through the library, seeing the shelves of scrolls. Each shelf was detailed with a description. Some were focused on architecture. Others weaponry, history, technology, societal science, oceanography, cosmology, artistry, and spirituality. Serilda watched as Vance gazed at the shelves.

"If you're behavior like this over some scrolls, I can only imagine your reaction to the Science Hall."

"Science Hall?"

"Follow me."

He followed Serilda down another set of corridors, taking them to the northwest portion of the palace where the Science Hall remained. The doors were opened as Vance saw the technology without haste. The walls were layered with the energy guns. All in the shapes of handguns, rifles, machine guns, and even Gatling guns. Also on the wall were hung swords, staves, javelins, axes, maces, and three tridents. Each one a different design than the other. Serilda began to describe to him the purpose of the hall and how the technologists each operate within the hall unaware of those in or out of the palace. While she showed Vance around, a guard stepped forward at the entrance, calling for Serilda.

"Yes?"

"Your father requires your presence at the throne room."

"I'm on my way."

The guard made his leave as Serilda told Vance to continue looking around. He wouldn't have to worry about a thing with Serilda speaking for him. Serilda had left and Vance walked through the hall. Seeing the weapons and further through the hall, he saw the structure which he knew would be used to layer out the ships for the Navy. Further down, he caught the glimpse of something larger. Entering the hall, spotting the ceiling inching higher than before. Vance looked and saw his ship sitting in the larger room.

"How did they find this?"

Vance ran toward the ship and looked at it. The ship was polished. No cracks. No broken glass. The ship was restored. Vance stepped up the ladder and pressed the ignition and the ship activated. The ship was fully repaired. Vance took the moment to think. Now he can return to Earth. Vance looked ahead in the ship's targeted direction, seeing a pathway which led to the outside of the palace. The ship could take off and make the escape from there. Vance took the second to conjure a plan. While he planned his next move, the Captain of the Hybrids arrived in the city with his hybrids and they quickly made haste toward the palace. Clashing against the guards at every turn. Kharan is warned of their arrival as he spoke with Serilda. Kharan stood up from his throne and snatched his staff from the side of the seat.

"Remain in here until it is clear."

"Yes, Father."

Kharan's Navy battled the Captain and his hybrids during the nightfall as the people of the city slept. That is until they heard the bells gong and they awoke to the sound of battle cries and clashing swords. The people began to evacuate from the city and head into the country land, which was set outside of the city's jurisdiction. Some chose to evacuate by jumping into boats of their own. While they did, they were caught in a stumble as Calypso and her crew made their return. Jumping from their ship into the battle. Calypso moved with fierce as she searched the surroundings for the Captain. Unable to find him on the outside, she turned her focus toward the palace and made her steps there. Inside the science hall, Vance could hear the sounds of the battle taking place as he looked back and forth between his ship and the sounds of the swords.

CHAPTER 8: THE VANOKIAN PATH

The battles continued outside between the hybrids, Calypso's pirates, and Kharan's Navy Guards. Meanwhile, inside the palace. Kharan waited in the gardens as the Captain of the Hybrids arrived. Moving with speed as he stopped himself, seeing the King. The Captain stepped forward into the garden. Seeing the plants growing across the walls, as if they were hung there from the start. The Captain pointed and scoffed.

"Must be some work to get this done."

"Why are you here?"

"Why am I here? Because I'm looking. Looking for a friend of mine. The Jarokian."

"The Jarokian is here under my authority. What do you seek with him?"

"Um, what do I seek? Uh, a chance to speak with him. Tell him to choose his path."

"What path?"

"Simple. He can either come with me and help the hybrids reclaim their territory or he can remain with you and eventually die under your rule."

"The Jarokian can handle himself. I've seen it firsthand."

"So, he can fight!" The Captain yelled. "That's even better. I knew he had it in him!"

Kharan slammed his staff into the ground and quickly before the Captain's sights, the staff transformed into a trident. The trident sparked with lightning as thunder roared from above.

"Such legends are true I see."

"Leave my palace!" Kharan yelled. "Take your hybrids with you before I have them all killed."

"Good sir, they are well prepared to die. Just as I."

The Captain's rapier clashed against Kharan's trident as the lightning traveled across weapons, shocking the Captain's hand. Kharan grinned as he twirled the trident and struck it into the ground, causing the lightning to move with speed and strike at the Captain's feet. He jumped over the bolts before they turned back toward him. He grabbed his rapier and scrapped the ground, taking the lightning onto his blade and holding it out toward Kharan.

"I know a few tricks as well."

The two faced off as Calypso rushed into the garden, seeing them staring down with both weapons pointed. She screamed for the Captain as she ran toward him with sword in hand. The Captain moved out of her path as Kharan threw his trident toward the Captain. He looked back and ducked own as the trident struck into the marble wall. He laughed.

"Two against one?! That's not fair. You need help."

The three of them looked at each other. The trident bolted back as the Captain ducked quickly, seeing the trident return to Kharan's hand. The Captain never seen a weapon do such a thing and took his leave. Calypso ran after him. While she chased him, Vance entered the battle, clashing against the guards and aiding the hybrids. Calypso saw him and anger fueled her as she ran toward him.

"You help them?!"

"I have to. It must be done."

"You choose the path of the Majority! For what cause have you grown such a hatred for yourself?!"

"It's not hatred. It's honesty."

"Then you know I have to kill you."

"I know you'll try. But, this night will not e the time."

Calypso glared toward Vance as the sound of an explosion shook the city. Calypso turned back, seeing how the explosion erupted from the palace as she ran inside. The guards followed as the hybrids made their escape. Vance escorted them back to their ship as he saw the Captain retreating from the palace. He rushed toward him.

"The Jarokian still lives!"

"What just happened?"

"I set off something that might get their attention. I see you are helping my crew."

"I am."

"Then you are with us?"

"I am."

"Then get onboard! Before the guards return."

Vance jumped onto the ship as they made their escape. The following morning, the city streets were filed with dead guards, pirates, and hybrids. Kharan called for a search for Vance, believing him to have been taken by the Captain. Although, Calypso's words urged him to find Vance and kill him since she believes he was the cause for the explosion. Serilda stood back and watched the conversation between her father and Calypso. While they spoke, the guards entered.

"My King. You have visitors."

"Visitors?" Kharan said with confusion. "Bring them in."

At the entrance to the throne room came three men. Dressed in fine robes of silver. Their eyes were as pale as the moon and their demeanor was one of a foreign stature. They bowed before Kharan, showing him reverence.

"Who are you?"

"We come from a place afar. We seek someone who is here unwillingly and uninvited."

"Who do you speak of?" Calypso asked.

"We know of the Jarokian. Of how he came on this planet and the actins he's done. We even know of his blasphemous believes toward the gods."

"Just why are you searching fro him?" Kharan wondered.

"Because he is a disruption to the balance. He must be found before the dark forces of Vanok arise and consume you all."

"How do the three of you know all of this?" Calypso questioned. "Where are you from?"

"Again, we're from a place afar. Find the Jarokian before the dark forces begin to return."

The three robed ones left the throne room, leaving Kharan and Calypso lost for words. Meanwhile, Vance stood out on the deck of the ship as they headed out into the open seas. The Captain walked over toward him, holding a map.

"Where are we headed?" Vance asked.

"A little place south of Aphro. There's some things there that must be done."

"I understand."

Vance looked out toward the sea and nodded. He knew he would be on Vanok for a while. A new life. A new adventure awaited.

NEW ORDER OF THE WORLD: AN EVERWAR UNIVERSE STORY

A corridor confined with metallic walls. Silent. Streams of white smoke emit from the steel-plated floors and ceiling. Down the hallway, the echoing sounds of tapping. The tapping morphed into beating and through the smoke a young man who is called Timothy. Dressed in all black with a long sleeve shirt and jeans. Wearing boots. Timothy is sweating and is running in the sight of fear. His life at the present moment is depending on his speed. Behind him we see four silhouettes after him. The silhouette later manifest into a guard. They're known as the Realm Guards. Soldiers of the City and loyal to their leader. Donned in black armored uniforms, carrying high-powered artillery firearms diverse from single ranges to plasma-ranges, weapons similar to the rainshockers of the Viper Realm. Their faces shrouded by their black masks and goggles. Resembling reapers. No emotion can be seen from them. They chase down Timothy through the corridor. Timothy keeps running and stops at a nearby room. He enters the room as quickly as he could run. Timothy took a small moment to catch his breath. Though, he can still hear the footsteps of the guards coming near the room. Timothy looked around and found himself in the presence of a robot. The robot is modeled after human structure, equipped with the A.I. from the technologies in the land. The name of the robot is A14-12.

"You appear to be in a rush."

"The Realm Guards are after me." Timothy said, catching his

breath. "I need to get rid of them."

"Now why would I assist you?"

"To keep them from killing me."

The robot examined Timothy and his garments.

"You're one of them."

Timothy nodded quickly. A14-12 recognized his intentions.

"Give me a moment."

Timothy waits for A14-12 to assist him, hearing the footsteps of the guards growing. Inching near him. Sweat drops from Timothy's forehead.

"They're coming closer!"

"Have some patience with me. After all, your kind know of patience."

A14-12 approaches Timothy with a device. The robot hands it to him. Timothy looks at it, unknown to what it is. He looks over at A14-12, questioning.

"What is this?" Timothy waved.

"If you want to evade the guards, hold it above your head."

Timothy scanned the device. Intrigued by its design.

"Is this some kind of teleporter?"

"No. They don't place them within this room. What you're holding will be good enough for your sudden cause."

The guards are near as their voices can be heard in the distance. Timothy holds the device above his head. A silver-colored mist fell from the device around him. Timothy notices himself becoming transparent. His flesh vanishing before his eyes. He knows he's becoming invisible. The guards burst into the room. Guns in hand. They circle the room, seeing only A14-12 standing. Calm demeanor for a robot. One guard approaches him. Eyes locked on tight.

"Mechroid, have you seen an enashian run past here?"

"I have not. You're the first I've seen this day."

"If you encounter the enashian, alert the Highguard."

"I will do that."

The guards leave the room and move further down the corridor. A14-12 looked around, scanning the room. Through the scanning process, the robot could see the invisible Timothy standing against the wall.

"Ah. There you are."

The robot grabbed a small firearm from the table and fired an electric bolt toward Timothy. The bolt hits Timothy in his left knee. He jolts and becomes visible again with the electric currents revealing himself.

"Why did you do that?!"

"You didn't make yourself visible, so I had to do it."

Timothy shook his head with a slight nod.

"Thanks."

Its not a problem. But, since you're here and finding your way out of this land. I assume you're on your way to finding the other renegades.

"The others?" Timothy jolted, waving his hands in disagreement. "No. No. I'm just trying to get out of this place with what I know."

"But, you're an enashian."

Timothy paused . The mechroid is aware Timothy isn't understanding the meaning of his words.

It's better of you to find them. You can lead them here to save the enashians and mechroids from the tyranny we live under.

"Why are you so interested in all of this?"

"I have my own reasons."

Timothy takes it in. Seeing what appears to be some form of character within the robot. A care perhaps? Unsure as to where the renegades may be.

"I'm on my way out of here anyway." Timothy let out a faint sigh. "I'll try to find the renegades."

"Maybe they'll find you."

"I'll take your word for it."

Timothy walks toward the door.

"We'll see once I get back. If I make it back."

"You'll be well." A14 said with certainty.

Timothy had left the room, running through the corridor and finding the exit. He exited the corridor and continued running.

Timothy runs outside of the base, he looks around, seeing himself surrounded by techno-buildings and flying drones made of beaten down metals. The buildings were as tall as skyscrapers and the air was lukewarm. The sounds of an electrical howling can be heard roaming in the skies above him. The city itself was one with great heaviness and astounding beauty. The structure looked to have been built many years ago. The aging itself had no greater effect than to instill fear. Its scent was of a burning fire mixed with electricity and a strange catch of cinnamon. He could hear the faint, yet squealing sounds of humans screaming coming from within the city. Their screams were of torment. It irked him, making his escape and finding himself entering the wilderness.

Timothy walks through the wilderness, known to those around the area as the Desolate. Nothing can be seen but a vast desert. Sand and rocks sit in places. Trees little to none. Few cactuses stood apart form each other. Scattered. Timothy walks through the Desolate as the wind slowly picks up and dust flies through the air. Timothy covers his face with his arm to avoid having sand fly into his eyes, nose, and mouth. He keeps walking as the wind increases in strength. The heat has increased in temperature and it begins to tire Timothy out. Yet, he continues moving through. After walking several more feet from his previous location, Timothy appears to spot a small structure up ahead.

"Is that a base?" Timothy glared.

As he goes to take another step, Timothy is stopped and lassoed from behind. Timothy looks down at the lasso around his torso. Hearing what is someone running toward him from behind, he turns his head, only to see a fist flying towards him. The fist punches Timothy, knocking him unconscious. Timothy awoke with a jolt. Beginning to regain his senses. Now knowing he's sitting down and his arms tied behind the chair. He's aware he's sitting in the middle of a room. The room is dark and the only light source he can see is coming from the sun above him through a circular hole in the ceiling. The room, of what Timothy could see was dirty with the Desolate sand. It smelled of vehicular oil and sweat. Its odor bothered Timothy, but he kept himself focused. Timothy tried looking around the room, seeing no one. He questions the scenario. He's tied up, so there must be someone within the room with him.

"OK." Timothy looked around. "This is strange. Anyone in here?"

No sound of a reply returns to him. Timothy quieted himself. Taking in a breath.

"Hello! Is there anyone in here besides me?! I'm pretty sure there is!"

Footsteps are heard in front of Timothy. Though, he cannot see who's walking as they are shrouded in the thick darkness surrounding him. The footsteps come closer and more footsteps are heard. They are surrounding Timothy and he knows it. Shaking around in the chair to set himself free. A voice comes through the darkness facing him.

"No need for you to do such a thing." A voice echoed.

Timothy stops shaking and stares into the darkness. Looking for the location of the voice. Squinting his eyes.

"Who's there? Speak again."

The footsteps are heard once more. Only this time, Timothy can see the boots coming into the light and after several more steps, Timothy can see the one who spoke to him. A middle-aged man. Rugged in appearance, wearing cargo attire with a sleeveless shirt with scruffy facial hair and a almost shaved head. The man was the leader of the Renegades.

"Here I am."

Timothy looked. Seeing Castle in front of him. From all around Timothy and Castle enter into the light the other renegades. About a dozen of them.

"As you can see, you're not alone."

"Why am I tied to this chair?"

"Few of the watch guards caught you roaming through the Desolate, alone. They believed you to be a shell for the realm guards. You're not one of them are you?"

"I am not one of them." Timothy replied.

"Your uniform represents the Realm. Therefore, it makes you a loyal subject to the Dictator."

Timothy gazed down at his uniform. He even looked around, scanning the renegades' own attire. He knew they could tell the difference between the ones who are aligned with the Dictator and those who are the renegades. The apparel of the renegades were cargo pants and militaristic vests. Both dirty and wet from water.

"I see your reasoning, Mr.?"

"Just call me Castle. I would like to know your intent of running through the Desolate alone."

"I was told that I could find you out here. Maybe convince you to help free the others trapped in the City."

"Is that right?"

"It is." Timothy glared at the Renegades. "I can guess by your questioning that you're the leader.

"I am. Been leading the renegades ever since the fall of our freedom came to pass.

"I can see they trust you."

"Damn right they can. Most of them I been with me through the battles. Lost friends and loved ones along the way. Yet, together we stand tall."

Timothy nodded. Castle searched him, seeing if he could learn

Timothy's motives.

"Tell me why you're here? Honestly."

"I escaped the confines of the City and ran into the Desolate. That's how your watch guards spotted me. I was told to find renegades by a mechroid."

Castle looked intrigued. Crossing his arms.

"What kind of mechroid?"

"An espionage mechroid. Operated with the technology within the City."

"Did it have a name?"

"Yeah."

"Tell me its name."

"That's not important. I can attest to that."

Castle stared at Timothy. His arms steady. No movement and little emotion.

"Why?"

"Try me."

Timothy nodded.

"A14-12. That was its name."

Castle looked over at the other renegades. They turned and spoke to each other before Castle focused his attention back to Timothy. Timothy could see the seriousness in Castle's eyes. Castle bent down toward Timothy, looking him in the eyes. Timothy shook with a certain fear. Castle's presence was something to fear. Even some of the renegades feared him.

"Where is this mechroid now?"

"Still in the City."

Castle grinned.

"I'm not certain to take what you've told me as fact."

"It's all true. That's the only reason I'm in this chair right now!"

"The only question is how could we enter the City when it is guarded by their snipers?"

"I…" Timothy shook. "I know a way inside the City."

"No shit." Castle scoffed.

"What I meant to say is I can take you and your group to the City. Sneak into the city and we can free the others."

Castle shook his head. Timothy couldn't tell if he accepted or rejected what he had told him. Castle stood in front of Timothy and cocked his head.

"How can we trust you?

"You can trust me. I'm not a betrayer."

"We'll know eventually. But, right now, we'll make our move into the City. And you'll be leading us in."

Timothy jerked with haste. Rattling the chair.

"Me? I don't understand?"

I'm not giving you the opportunity of bringing myself and my soldiers into death."

Timothy paused himself.

"I see your reasoning.

"That's a good start."

Castle reaches on the side of his leg and pulls out a knife. Timothy stops moving as Castle takes the knife and cuts the ropes from Timothy and the chair. Timothy sighs with relief as he stands up slowly from the chair. Castle takes the knife and places it onto Timothy's throat. Timothy gulped.

"Because if you wrong us in any way. I will personally kill you. Do you understand?"

"I understand."

Castle smiled, placing the knife back into his pocket.

"Good to know."

Castle looks to the renegades. He nods with a smirk on his face. The renegades rally up and equip themselves with their weapons, ranging from energy guns, plasma grenades, knives, and energy-coated knives." Timothy sees them gathering their weapons. Feeling uneasy as he's just walking through the area.

Outside of the base, the renegades are sitting on dirt bikes, preparing to ride off toward the Realm's City. Timothy himself gets onto a bike. Castle sees him on the bike and points at him.

"You get in the front!" Castle pointed outward.

"You and your soldiers have the firepower." Timothy replied. "Why do I have to be in the front?"

"Get your ass in the front!"

Timothy went and sat atop the bike in front of them. Castle gave the renegades the command to follow.

The renegades had reached the city. They paused for a moment and Castle turns over to Timothy. Pointing at the city. Glancing up to the skyscraper structure and moving crafts.

"Lead us in."

"Of course. Follow along quietly. Hide your bikes over near the walls. The guards rarely do searches on this side of the city."

"Hide the bikes." Castle commanded the Renegades.

The renegades leave their bikes next to the wall. The wall is made up of a mixture between bricks and titanium wiring. The wiring glowed various colors with electricity flowing through it. It appears as if it was meant to be a twisted, yet somewhat beautiful sight to outsiders. Timothy guided Castle and the renegades toward the location where he had exited the city during his escape. The surroundings were clear as Timothy opened the door and they entered into the corridor.

Castle walked behind Timothy while the other renegades watched every corner. Prepared to fire.

"I have to ask you, kid. Why are you involved in all of this?"

"It's all a mistake." Timothy answered.

"A mistake? Saving others from tyranny is no mistake."

Timothy stops and faces Castle. Castle reads his eyes. He senses something within him. Hidden behind his outward visage.

"I see. You're a deserter."

Timothy took note and continued walking.

"You turned against the Realm and for good reason."

"I turned against them because of the destruction they plan to bring."

"They've always plotted destruction. It's nothing new."

"Be that as it may. It doesn't spare me from the death I will receive."

"Death is only a solution of theirs. To trigger fear. What you've done, whether it is out of cowardice or bravery, it's for a greater cause."

Timothy listened to Castle's words closely.

"Hope I don't screw it up."

"You won't. You've shown me enough to figure that."

Walking through the corridor slowly, Timothy returned to the room A14-12 was in. Timothy enters the room with a storming haste.

The electric room is the base for the City's primary grid system. The walls glowing with a bluish hue as the energy flows through the wiring. Timothy looks around the room, but A14-12 is nowhere to be seen. Castle enters the room and looks around. Seeing the amount of tech that sat within its walls.

Castle scanned the room entirely. His eyes keen to the doorways.

"Look at this stuff."

Timothy looked over toward Castle. Shaking his head. Castle doesn't understand what Timothy's problem is or what he's trying to say.

"What is it?"

"The mechroid isn't here."

"Maybe it went to help the others find a way out."

"Maybe."

Not finding the mechroid, Timothy led them outside of the electric room.

As they step out into the corridor, on the other end are realm guards. Staring down Timothy, Castle, and the renegades. Their energy guns are searing and buzzing. Prepared for fire.

"Well, I'll be damned. We have company."

One of the realm guards raised up his plasma-range.

"Renegades! You have one request. Surrender yourselves now and come with us to be questioned and judged."

Castle stood firm. Determined about his next move as were the Renegades.

"I'm not going anywhere with you."

"We will now respond in the proper circumstance."

Castle stood his ground with the renegades. The realm guards begin firing toward the renegades. They run across the corridor. Some enter the electric room. Castle fires back at the guards with the renegades. Flying energy blasts zooming across the corridor back and forth. Timothy ran out of the corridor and into another doorway, which led down into another corridor.

Timothy ran through the second corridor and as he reaches its end, he bumps into A14-12. Standing around the robot are humans, beaten and battered, looking to escape. Timothy smiled.

"Where were you earlier?"

"I was preparing to aid these people for escape."

"How would you get them out?"

"I knew you were coming back with the renegades."

"How?" Timothy asked.

"I have my ways."

Timothy nods and leads them out of the corridor and toward the exit. He opens the door and the people barge out of the corridor.

"Get away from this place as far as you can."

The people run outside and towards the Desolate. Timothy and A14 return to the first corridor, where they can hear the echoes of firing energy blasts. Nearing the doorway, the blasts slowly cease and turn into silence. Timothy, hesitant to open the door, opens it anyway. Timothy and A14 enter the first corridor and within the corridor are dead renegades and dead guards. They look and see Castle with several other renegades exit the electric room. Castle smiles and laughs as he approaches Timothy and A14.

"Where did you go?"

"I helped A14 set some humans free." Timothy looked around. "I see that you've managed to take them out."

"As you can see, I lost some of my own. Enough as I can manage at the moment."

Timothy turned to A14 as did Castle.

"We must leave this place now. She's coming."

"Who's coming?" Timothy wondered.

Castle shakes his head looking at Timothy as they proceed to exit the corridor and return to the outside.

"You mean to tell me that you don't know who "she" is?"

Timothy stood confused.

"I don't know who A14 is talking about. Who is this "she"?"

"We must hurry."

"Who is she?" Timothy asked.

They approach the exit door and open it. Running to the outside of the City.

Running outside, they find themselves chased by drones and several realm guards. Castle sees it and isn't happy about it. His face twists with anger and haste.

"Damn!" Castle yelled.

"This isn't good."

"You don't say."

A14 starts to beep as they get on the bikes. The mechroid can sense someone approaching them near the realm guards. A14 knows of that peculiar presence.

"Here she comes."

"I'm asking, who is she?"

Castle turned to face the guards. It was there he saw her in the distance. The footsteps sounded rough against the dirt. With vigor.

"Look ahead, kid." Castle pointed.

Timothy looks and see her. A woman dressed in all grey. Her dark hair down to her shoulders. Her eyes glowing of emerald. He lips red as blood. Her countenance as wicked as one could read. She is the Dictator.

They ride off into the Desolate as realm guards approach the Dictator. Bowing before her presence.

"Should we pursue them, my Lady?"

"No need." The Dictator grinned. "Everything is in proper order."

The realm guards returned to the City while the Dictator stared, watching the bikes ride out further into the Desolate.

AN EXCERPT FROM MARK PORTER OF ARGORON

CHAPTER 1: THE INCIDENT

United States Army Lieutenant, Mark Porter is currently on a mission to Roswell, New Mexico. His focus is keen as he traveled alone, listening to musical instrumentals. As he drove, his cell phone rings and he answers it.

"Lieutenant Porter." he said.

"Porter, this is General Dunlap." the caller said. "How far are you from the site?"

"I'm looking at it as we speak." Porter said.

Porter drove to the entrance gate, where two soldiers stood. They opened the gate , permitting him entry. Porter recognized the location, while still speaking with the General on the phone.

"General, I must ask, what is this place?"

"This is Area 51."

"Area 51." Porter intrigued. "I never thought I would be here."

"See you inside, Porter."

Porter hung up the phone, entering into the front entrance of the buildings. Area 51 had the appearance of a small city, with dozens of soldiers and officials moving throughout. Most of which are military soldiers and scientists. Porter stepped out of the car, heading towards the front doors layered with bulletproof glass. He entered, being greeted by soldiers. Porter took a left turn toward the elevator. Inside the elevator were two scientists.

"Excuse me, but are you Mark Porter?" one scientist asked.

"Yes I am."

"Its an honor to meet such a well-known Lieutenant." the other scientist said.

"Thank you."

The elevator had reached its destination floor. Porter is the first one to walk out, only to avoid the two scientists. Porter walked down a hallway and in the distance, he saw General Dunlap. Porter begins walking toward him. General Dunlap saw Porter coming down the hall near him.

"Porter, right on schedule."

"Yes sir, General."

Porter and General Dunlap entered another room. As they walked, Dunlap began telling Porter a few details to the secret operations being held within the facility. Porter took a guess to what it may be with only Dunlap smirking without saying a word.

"Porter, there are some rules that you must obey, since you're here."

"Ok, General. What are they?"

"You must not tell a single soul what you're about to see in this next room." Dunlap said. "If you do, we will have no choice but to rid you of the world."

"I see. Must be something very important."

"Important?" Dunlap said. "Try highly secretive. If anyone found out about this, the world will turn for the worst."

They reached the room and the metal door slowly slides open. The room was surrounded with military security. Little light was emitted into the room as the rest was covered in darkness. Porter gazed around, seeing scientists doing autopsies on unknown beings.

"General, what is going on here?" Porter asked.

"I'll tell you once we've reached our location."

Passing through the security, walking into yet another room. This room was lit up with plenty of light and wasn't nearly as shrouded in darkness like the other. Inside the room is a long table with a device sitting in the middle. Porter and Dunlap approached the table, looking at the device.

"Porter, this device you see here is able to transfer beings, human or not, to other worlds."

"Other worlds? Like planets?"

"Yes. Perhaps even dimensions are a possibility. Testing will only reveal how soon."

"How is that possible?" Porter asked. "Has it been tested?"

"Not yet. We're still awaiting an answer from the President."

They walked around the table, looking from all angles. The device was shiny, projecting a blue light which directed into the air. Porter slowly held his hand over the device before Dunlap snatched it from getting closer.

"You don't want to do something that you'll regret."

"Sorry, sir."

As they stood looking at the device, an alarm goes off. Porter and Dunlap look around. Dunlap ran toward the doors, questioning the security as to what triggered the alarm.

"What the hell's going on?!" Dunlap yelled.

"The base, sir, its under attack!" a soldier yelled.

"Porter, stay where you are!"

He pulled out his pistol, looking outside the door. From the outside, he saw soldiers and scientists being attacked by an unknown force. The opposing force appeared to have tentacles, while wearing peculiar white robes with long white hair extending to their lower back. Dunlap glared out of the glass window of the door, staring at them, watching them kill the soldiers and scientists. Gunshots are heard from the outside, but they're dying left and right.

Porter approached toward the door, but is stopped by Dunlap, who commanded Porter to stay by the table.

"General, what's going on?!"

"Sit tight, Lieutenant!" Dunlap said. "We're in for a show."

Dunlap backed from the door as it bursts open. He began shooting at the beings, but the gunshots have no effect. Porter takes out his revolver and shoots one of the beings in the head, which kills it. Dunlap looks at Porter, astounded.

"Try that, General."

"I surely will."

They both begin shooting the beings that are coming into the room through the damaged door. They aim for the head and shoot them directly there. They've killed the beings and look at each other. Both astounded and calm.

"Good job, Lieutenant."

"Same to you, General."

They shook hands, but from the ceiling a bright light shines down on them and Porter pushes Dunlap out of the way and a loud bang is heard with a large flash of light, nearly blinding Dunlap. The light fades away and Dunlap looks around for Porter.

"Porter?" Dunlap spoke. "Porter?!"

Dunlap looks around and realizes that Porter is nowhere in sight, but he also realized that the device's light is now dim, which before it was bright. He now knows that someone has happened to Porter.

Porter, who's opening his eyes, realizes that he's in a desert. He looks and stands up, brushing the dirt off of his uniform. He walks around the area, looking around at it surroundings.

"Where the hell am I?"

CHAPTER 2: CAPTIVE FOREIGNER

He continued walking, although realizing that he can move faster and jump higher than usual. Knowing now something isn't quite right. He continued to move ahead, but in front of him, he sees something running towards him. He tries to get a closer look and he sees that they looked human. He begins running the other direction, but is shot down by a bow and arrow. Porter lays on the ground as the beings get closer to him. He now hears silence, but the beings are surrounding him.

The beings appeared to be humans, yet there was a difference to them. Their skin was darker and their bodies were toned. They stared down Porter as he glared at them. They spoke to each other in an unknown language that Porter couldn't understand. He stood up, staggering from the arrow wound, stepping back from the beings and points to the one wearing white fur over his shoulders. His stature gave Porter to belief to be the general.

"You, where am I? Tell me where the hell I am?!"

The humanoids looked at Porter, their thoughts ponder if he's not from their world. One approached Porter and looks at him from all angles and stands back with his group. Porter stares at the group, reaching for his revolver, but he doesn't have it. He looks at what he perceived to be the humanoids' general and saw he had his revolver.

"How did you get that?!" Porter asked with rage. "Where am

I?!"

Porter walked over to the beings, but he's knocked unconscious by one of their punches. They dragged him back to their location, locking him up. Hours later, Porter awakens and is now chained to a rock with no way out. He sees the beings from before, but this time, there's more. Porter begins thinking that he may not be on Earth anymore. He know believes that he's somewhere else, somewhere unknown.

Porter tried to break himself out of the chains, but he's too tired and weary to do so. He looks around as he's surrounded by dirt and feces. He continues to look around to find an object that could break him out of the chains. He doesn't find any tools that he could use, so he sits in the dungeon through the entire night. The next day, he awakens and sees himself surrounded by the tall, green beings. One in particular, releases him of the chains and helps him up, Porter stares at the being and looks into its eyes.

"What are you?" Porter asked.

"We are the Micrans." The being said. "Warriors of Argoron."

"What...? Argoron? Where am I?"

"You are on Argoron, stranger."

"Argoron?' Porter said. 'Where is that? I've never heard of Argoron.'

"If you're not from here, then, where do you come from?.' The being said. "What is your origin?"

"I'm not understanding what you mean? Where exactly am I?"

"You're on Argoron. A planet in the vastness of the stars."

"Argoron?" Porter questioned. "No. I was just in New Mexico."

"Where do you come from? Truly?"

"My name is Mark Porter." Porter said. "."

From the entrance came the leader of this particular warrior clan, Saban Jai. Saban walked toward and stood in front of Porter. Porter stared, not knowing what to expect.

"Mark Porter." Saban said. "How can you be from Jagoron?"

"What? No, I'm from Earth, not Jagoron? What is a Jagoron?"

"That is what I said, Mark Porter of Jagoron The world you come from is called Jagoron in this land. To your species, the earth-walkers, Jagoron is called Earth."

Porter sat confused. The Micrans didn't know what to make of his reaction. Saban didn't bother with him, rallying the others to bring him to the carriage. The carriage seemed to be made of a reddish wood as were the wheels, decorated with spears and red flags with no markings. Two of the Micrans carried Porter into the carriage, which was pulled by two eight-legged creatures. Which Porter saw them, he immediately thought them to be horses. However, he spotted they each had two tails and two sets of eyes on both sides. Speaking the word, Saban chuckled.

"Moreks." Saban said. "That's what they are. The fastest beasts in all of Argoron."

Saban jumped into the front of the carriage, gaining control over the horses as they rode off from the vast desert toward the massive metropolitan city as they approached the gates of the city of *Taranopolis*, as the inhabitants called it. Porter took a look outside of the carriage, seeing the massive city with its pointed skyscrapers and layered structures. The vehicles which moved throughout the city were a mix of the carriage and anti-gravity ships. The ships appeared to have four sets of transparent wings in the colors of rubies. The sky above the city was orange with a hint of red. The city was surrounded by red flags, flowing calmly with the wind throughout the city as the temperature was warm enough to have the people dressed in light clothing. Some even glanced at Porter, seeing his attire. From there, Porter knew he was out of place, especially when glancing upward toward the ships.

"Where am I?" Porter asked himself.

The carriage stopped in front of the city's palace. The Micrans stood by the carriage door, dragging Porter to the outside as they entered the palace. Porter stood on his feet, being held by two Micran soldiers, walking toward what he guessed was the throne room. In the room, Porter saw three chairs. Two were empty and the center one was full as there was a man sitting, speaking with another man. The man standing up had the wings of a dragon folded on his back and claws for fingers. Dressed in armored leather. The man sitting down was decked in armor, linen, and fur. On his head sat a crown made of what appeared to be gold or bronze. Porter couldn't make out any of it, yet, he knew they were royalty in their own way.

"You know why I've come and visited you, my lord."

"Yes, I am aware of your need for warriors. As of right now, there aren't many who are at my disposal for combat."

"What of your prisoners? What use will you have for them other than wasting away behind cell doors?"

The one in the chair nodded, rubbing his chin.

"You have a point."

They looked toward the entrance, seeing the Micrans carrying Porter. The man standing pointed and his yellow eyes widen. The man in the seat stood up, glaring toward the Micran warriors and the prisoner they held.

"A new prisoner?"

"My lord." Saban said, kneeling. "We have another prisoner in need of interrogation."

The man stared at Porter, seeing his clothing and his tone. He was uncertain of Porter's ethnicity to his own and the others around him. He turned back to Saban, raising his hand, giving him the order to stand.

"And what has this man done and what is he wearing?"

"We're not sure, sire. He was dressed in this manner when we found him."

"And where did you find him?"

"Out in the wilderness. He appeared dazed. Confused you

might say. He was speaking strangely, so we brought him here. To get more answers. If you request it, my king."

The King nodded.

"Very well. Take him to the room. Ivo will be there to get any answers we may need."

"And what of him after you received your answers?" The other man said.

"When the time comes, I will call to you, Wyvern King. Right now, best you return to your domain. Prepare your warriors for the entertainment of the masses."

"I will keep my eyes and ears open."

The Wyvern King's wings buckled as he nodded his head, walking toward the exit. The King looked back, seeing Saban and the warriors leading Porter into the interrogation room. He sighed as he sat down and from the entrance arrived a young woman, dressed in a silver dress and long reddish-orange hair. She bowed before the king and he smiled.

"My daughter. I see you've returned from your journey."

"I have, father. I also have some news regarding the people of the city."

"News? What kind of news?"

"The people are aware of the coming war with the Celedians."

"And how do they know this?"

"Some have described a strange man coming into the city, warning them of the war and giving them the choice to choose which side they're on."

"A speaker of war in my city." The King said. "I see I must find him. Or, perhaps Saban has already brought him in."

The Princess wasn't sure what her father had meant. He chuckled and stood up, walking toward his daughter.

"Let me handle the matters of war. You must prepare for a wedding. Saban is a good man and a future leader."

"I... I understand."

The King looked at his daughter as she let out a small smile.

"I have other matters to attend to. Make sure you keep yourself protected when you're out in the city."

"The guardsmen will stand by me."

"Good, my Arribel."

CHAPTER 3: WHO ARE YOU?

Porter struggled against the strength of the two Micrans as they chained his wrists to the wall before exiting. Porter stared quietly, hearing footsteps approaching the cell. The door had opened for Porter to glance at two other warriors and a peculiar following the middle. He stood about the height of Porter, but he was much older as his white hair could attest.

"Who are you?"

"What?" Porter said slowly.

"Who are you? What is your name?"

"My name is Mark Porter."

"Mark Porter." Ivo said. "Strange name. never heard of such a one. Tell me, Mark Porter, where are you from?"

"I'm not from here. So, that's a start."

"Your name tells me all I need to know. Why have you come here, Mark Porter? Are you a spy for the Celedians? The Ceruleanians? Orgons, perhaps?"

"What are you talking about? I'm not from this place. "

"Your physical tells the tale. You're a warrior."

"I'm a soldier. A lieutenant."

"Convenient." Ivo chuckled. "And you've come here for what purpose other than being a spy or an invader?"

"I am not an invader nor am I some kind of spy. I didn't come here on my own accord. It's hard to explain. Even for myself. The place I come from is Earth. Earth is my home."

"Earth? You speak of Jagoron, the blue world where the waters move across the grounds."

"I guess you can detail it as much."

"Who sent you here?"

"I don't know."

"Then, start with something for me to go along. To understand your plight."

Porter sighed, waving his hands slight in a non-caring manner, yet, Porter began to tell Ivo of the encounter in Area 51, the ambush, and the instant transportation. Ivo listened closely to every word Porter had spoken. Once Porter had come to the conclusion of his sudden appearance in the desert, Ivo ceased him.

"You were brought here."

"Yes. But, I'm not sure by what or how."

"What is it you truly desire at this moment?"

"To be out of these chains and to be sent back home."

Ivo chuckled.

"There will be a time for that. Getting you back home however, is a tricky obstacle. For if you do not know how you came to Argoron, how does it make sense for you to find your way back."

"I saw the ships you people have. They're far beyond what I've seen. Now, I can take one of them and fly it back to Earth. A safe passage to get home."

"Enough." Ivo said, silencing Porter. "Our customs are far different than your kind. For one to achieve the freedom which one craves, they must earn it and win it."

"Win it? I'm not understanding."

"Combat. A trial to test your strength. To learn your endurance. Mentally. Physically. Spiritually. Only then will we and yourself see the conclusion to the whole matter."

"Are you telling me I must fight to get home?"

"Yes."

Porter sighed. Hanging his head low. He thought for a moment if this was only a dream. A hallucination, yet, with the small pain he felt in his legs, he knew it was real. All of it.

"I'm sorry. But, I am not going to be treated as some sort of amusement to you and your people here. I demand to be sent home."

Ivo turned back and walked toward the cell door. He opened it before taking a look back at Porter. Measuring him with a gaze.

"Your freedom demands on your fighting spirit. I hope you have one."

Ivo exited the cell, calling over a Micran guard. Ivo signaled the guard to keep watch of Porter's cell for the remainder of the day and throughout the night. Several hours later, nightfall fell over Taranopolis and the city was sleep. The sky which as glowing red had become as dark with glares and glistens of a peculiar bluish hue. Porter sat inside his cell. Barely ate the food they delivered to him. He looked over toward the guard sitting at the door. With the faint light shining from the window above him, Porter caught the glimpse of a key. Believing the key to be the only way out of his cell. Porter made a move, but remembered his wrists were attached to chains embedded into the concrete wall.

"Hey." Porter whispered. "Hey."

The guard jolted a bit, no movement afterwards. Porter sighed as he looked around the cell for something. Anything to get the guard's attention. Porter thought and glanced over to his left, seeing the tray of food. His eyes moved from the tray to the guard. Porter swiped his foot, kicking the tray against the cell doors, rattling up the guard as he jumped up with a sword in hand. Porter saw the blade.

"What's going on in there?" The guard asked.

"Water." Porter said. " I need water."

"Water? Where do you see any water?"

"To drink. I need something to drink."

The guard sighed and walked off, leaving Porter waiting. Unsure of what he could've waited for, the guard had returned, holding a small flask in his hand. He opened the cell door and entered, putting the flask on the ground as he unlocked the cuff from Porter's right wrist from the chain. Porter sighed and paused, quickly snatching he flask and smashing it into the guard's face before kicking the guard in the throat and stomping on his head. The helmet which the guard had word was cracked on the side. Porter looked to the guard's hand, seeing the key. He grabbed it and unruffled his left wrist. Being free from the wall, Porter grabbed the chest plate and helmet of the guard. Taking the sword last as he made his escape from the cell. Porter moved through the corridors quietly, avoiding other guards and even those who were playing a game of *L'agh*. In the distance, Porter saw the moonlight peaking from a doorway. Porter reached the door and found himself staring at the outside toward the vast desert. He sighed, knowing if he wanted to escape, going back into the desert was his only option. Porter made his move and ran out into the desert with only Argoron's moon as his source of direction.

MARK PORTER OF ARGORON

AVAILABLE NOW IN PAPERBACK AND E-BOOK

VANCE HARLAN, THE CAPTAIN AND THE HYBRIDS,
KING KHARAN, CALYPSO, AND SERILDA WILL
RETURN IN:

COMING IN 2022

ABOUT THE AUTHOR

Ty'Ron W. C. Robinson II is the author of several works of fiction. Including the *Dark Titan Universe Saga*, *The Haunted City Saga*, EverWar Universe, Symbolum Venatores, Frightened!, Instincts, and others. More information pertaining to the author and stories can be found at darktitanentertainment.com.

Twitter: @TyronRobinsonII

Twitter: @DarkTitan_
Instagram: @darktitanentertainment
Facebook: @DarkTitanEnt
Pinterest: @darktitanentertainment
YouTube: Dark Titan Entertainment

www.ingramcontent.com/pod-product-compliance
Lightning Source LLC
LaVergne TN
LVHW041538060526
838200LV00037B/1036